This dragon book belongs to:

....

Dragon and The Bully
My Dragon Books - Volume 5
Written by Steve Herman

Copyright © 2018 by Digital Golden Solutions LLC.
Published by DG Books Publishing, an imprint of Digital Golden Solutions LLC.

Information contained within this book is for entertainment and educational purposes only. Although the author and publisher have made every effort to ensure that the information in this book was correct at press time, the author and publisher do not assume and hereby disclaim any liability to any party for any loss, damage, or disruption caused by errors or omissions, whether such errors or omissions result from negligence, accident, or any other cause.

ISBN: 978-1948040143 (paperback)
ISBN: 978-1948040266 (hardcover)

www.MyDragonBooks.com

First Edition: March 2018

10 9 8 7 6 5 4 3 2 1

Once upon a time there lived a little boy named Drew...

Who had himself a dragon
by the name of Diggory Doo.

So Drew enrolled his dragon in a special kind of school.

Diggory learned to fly and keep his scales all shiny bright, And to get along with others and to try hard not to bite.

He learned to snap his tail
and make his face look very scary,
And never ever shoot a flame,
unless it's necessary!

When it came to learning lessons,
Diggory Doo was number one.

There was a dinosaur
by the name of Stinky Steve

Who bullied Diggory Doo
and did some things you won't believe!

Stinky Steve would cut in line and would not wait his turn...

He always laughed at Diggory Doo,
which wasn't very nice...

He poked him with a pencil
and had tripped him once or twice.

Stinky stomped on Diggory's tail,
then he kicked him in the knee...

One day Stinky set the teacher's desk on fire,

Then blamed the deed on Diggory Doo – Stinky was a liar!

Diggory Doo went home
and had a little talk with Drew;
Diggory told his friend
what he thought he ought to do.

Drew thought a while and then replied,
"I know that it's been tough,
And when it comes to Stinky Steve,
I'm sure you've had enough."

"May I suggest, to do what's best,
I think that you will find...
You get more satisfaction
when you respond by being **KIND**."

"If this is true," said Diggory Doo,
"I guess I must agree,
I should be nice to Stinky Steve,
although he's mean to me."

Stinky Steve was crying,
for he fell and skinned his knee,
And Diggory Doo remembered
that **kindness** was the key.

Although he could have laughed at him or kicked him while he's down, Diggory Doo decided to lift Stinky off the ground.

He dusted off the dirt
and wiped Stinky's tears away,

Then Diggory Doo asked Stinky Steve
if he would like to play.

Stinky Steve could not believe it!
He was so surprised!

Then Stinky Steve shocked Diggory Doo when he apologized!

Diggory Doo and Stinky Steve
had finally made amends;
And now they have become
the best of friends!

So if you know a bully and
you don't know what to do...
A little **kindness** just might work –
Just ask Diggory Doo!

Get your FREE Gift from Diggory Doo at
www.MyDragonBooks.com/gift

Read more about Drew and Diggory Doo!

POTTY TRAIN YOUR DRAGON
Steve Herman

TRAIN YOUR ANGRY DRAGON
Steve Herman

THE MINDFUL DRAGON
Steve Herman

THE YOGA DRAGON
Steve Herman

DRAGON & THE BULLY
Steve Herman

HAPPY BIRTHDAY DRAGON
Steve Herman

TRAIN YOUR DRAGON TO ACCEPT NO
Steve Herman

I GOT THIS!
Steve Herman

TRAIN YOUR DRAGON TO BE KIND
Steve Herman

A DRAGON With His Mouth ON FIRE
Steve Herman

TRAIN YOUR DRAGON To Follow RULES
Steve Herman

TRAIN YOUR DRAGON To Be RESPONSIBLE
Steve Herman

TRAIN YOUR DRAGON To LOVE HIMSELF
Steve Herman

TEACH YOUR DRAGON To Understand CONSEQUENCES
Steve Herman

TEACH YOUR DRAGON TO STOP LYING
Steve Herman

TEACH YOUR DRAGON TO MAKE FRIENDS
Steve Herman

Visit
www.MyDragonBooks.com
for more!

Made in the USA
Lexington, KY
05 May 2019